CUT&
COLOR
PLAYBOOK
CITIES

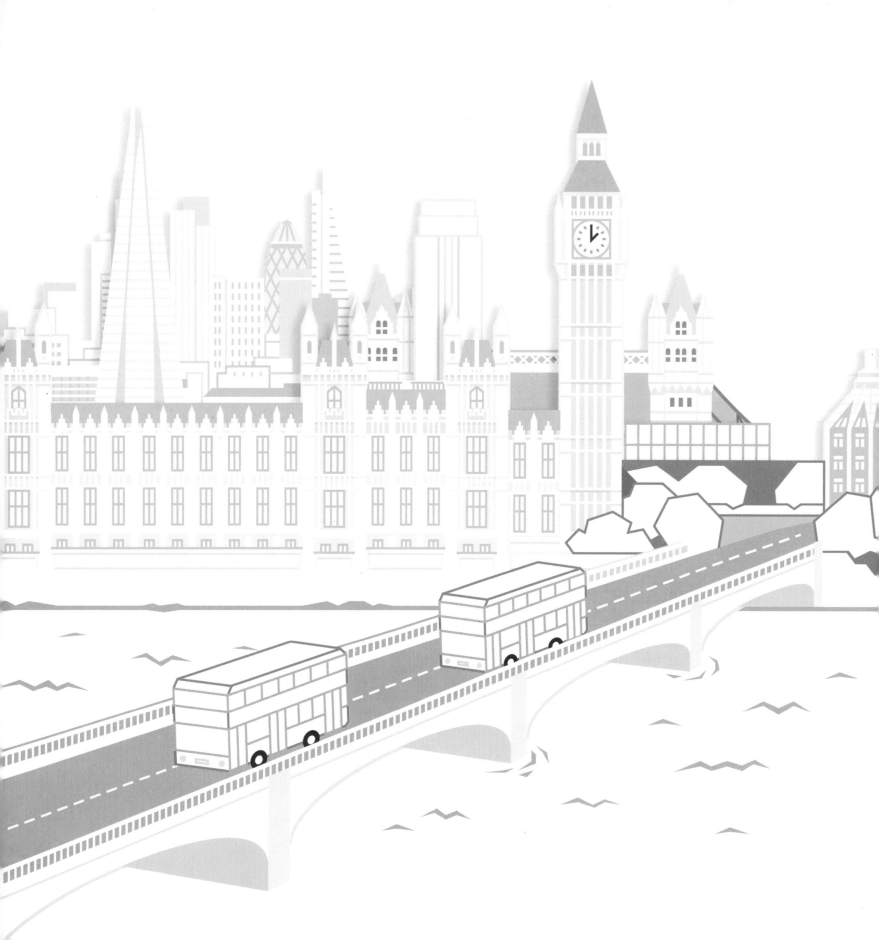

Cléa Dieudonné

CUT&
COLOR
PLAYBOOK
CITIES

Kane Miller
A DIVISION OF EDC PUBLISHING

Safety warning: Children should use craft scissors for the following
activities, and should be supervised by a responsible adult at all times.

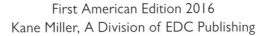

CONTENTS

HOW TO USE THIS BOOK

Color, cut and create four city scenes!

1 Follow the instructions to add color and detail to each scene.

2 Cut away the parts of the page that have a scissor pattern on the back.

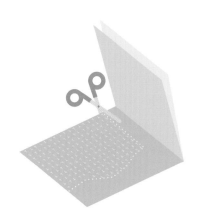

3 Once you have finished, flip back to the frame at the front to see the layered picture revealed! You can then try to spot the buildings and landmarks you have colored.

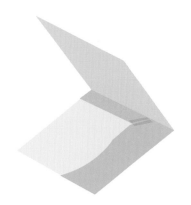

Tip: If you accidentally cut away the wrong part of the page, don't panic! Just fix it with some sticky tape on the back of the page.

HOW TO START

Poke your scissors into the hole that is already cut out on the frame page, and start cutting out the frame. Do this carefully to make sure that you don't accidentally cut into or break the frame. Write the name of each city at the bottom of the border.

Tip: Ask an adult to help you if you have trouble cutting out the frame.

7

LONDON

What a busy city! All kinds of buildings line the streets. Some are grand and very old. There are stores, offices, museums, hotels and houses.

Vroom! Vroom! There's so much to see as you travel around the city. Will you ride on a double-decker bus or in a black taxi?

It's raining today. People enjoy walking in the city but need umbrellas and waterproof clothes to keep dry.

e to the city!

our favorite

ake this frame

nd exciting.

utting here.

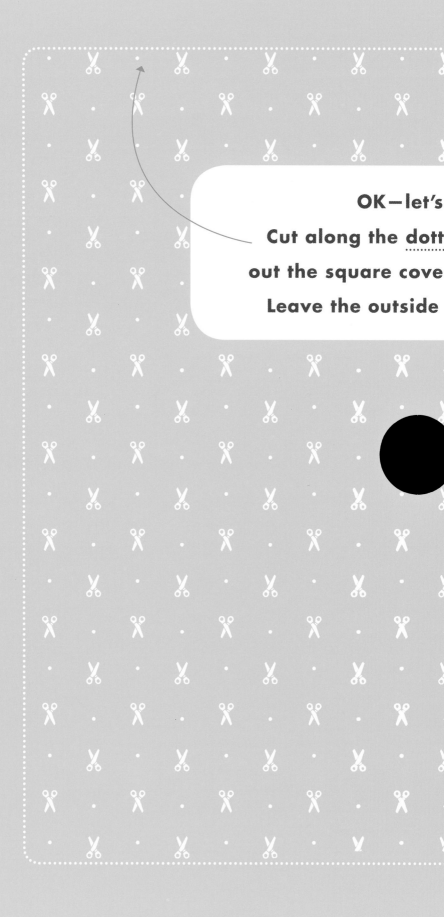

OK—let's
Cut along the dott
out the square cove
Leave the outside

Welcome to the city!

Choose your favorite

colors to make this frame

Start cutting here.

OK—let's go!

Cut along the **dotted line** to cut
out the square covered in scissors.
Leave the outside frame intact.

Vroom! This double-decker bus carries people all around the city. Color it bright red.

Cut along the dotted line.

Make this row of
grand houses bright
and cheerful.

Count all the front
doors. What colors
are they?

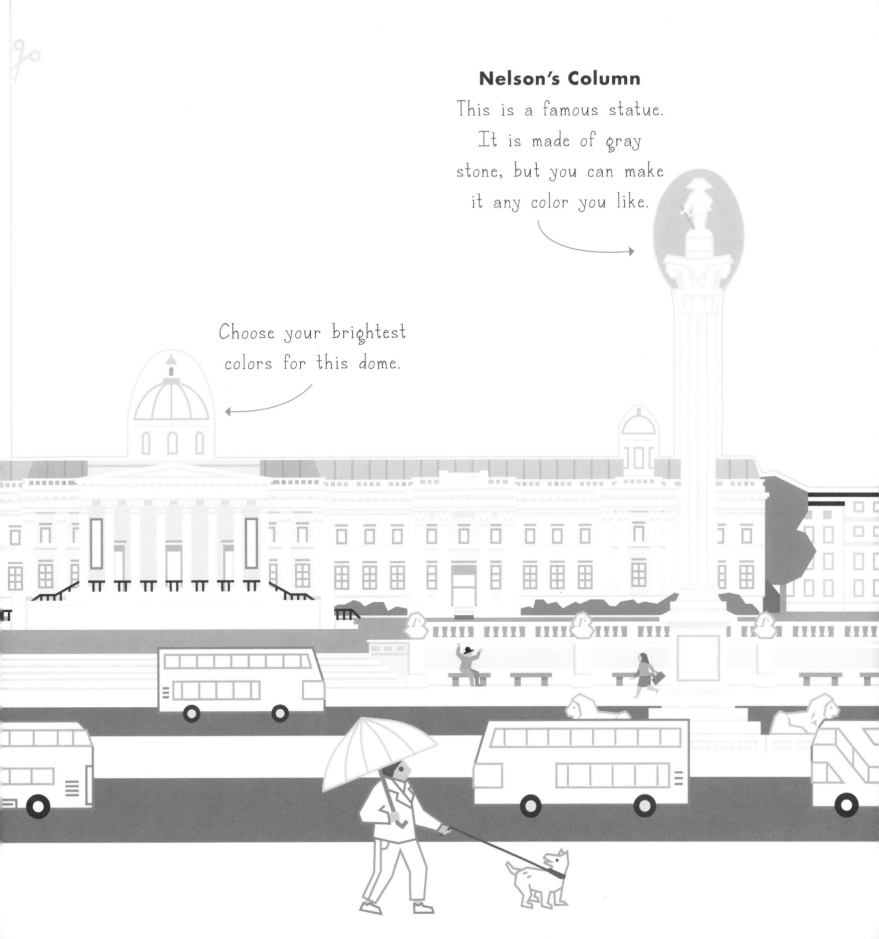

Nelson's Column
This is a famous statue.
It is made of gray
stone, but you can make
it any color you like.

Choose your brightest
colors for this dome.

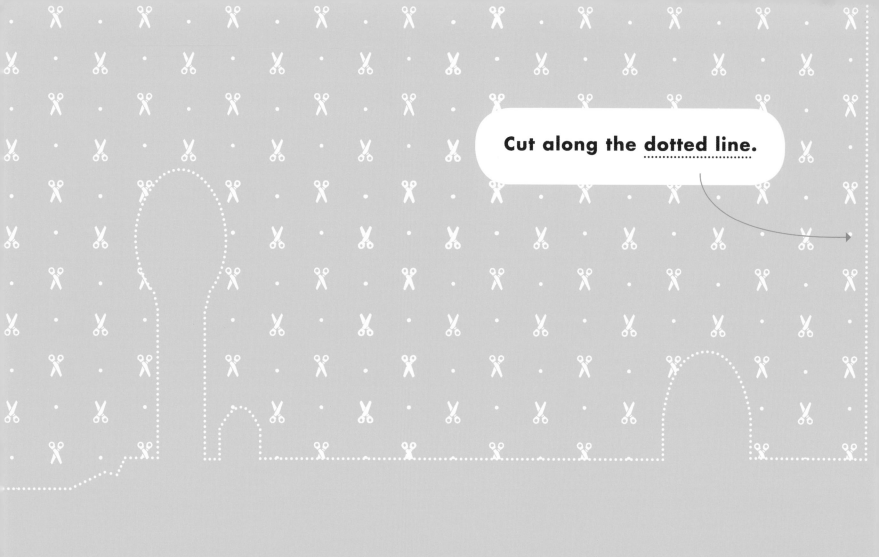

Cut along the dotted line.

These are advertising spaces.
Fill them with pictures, patterns
and rainbow colors.

Cut along the dotted line.

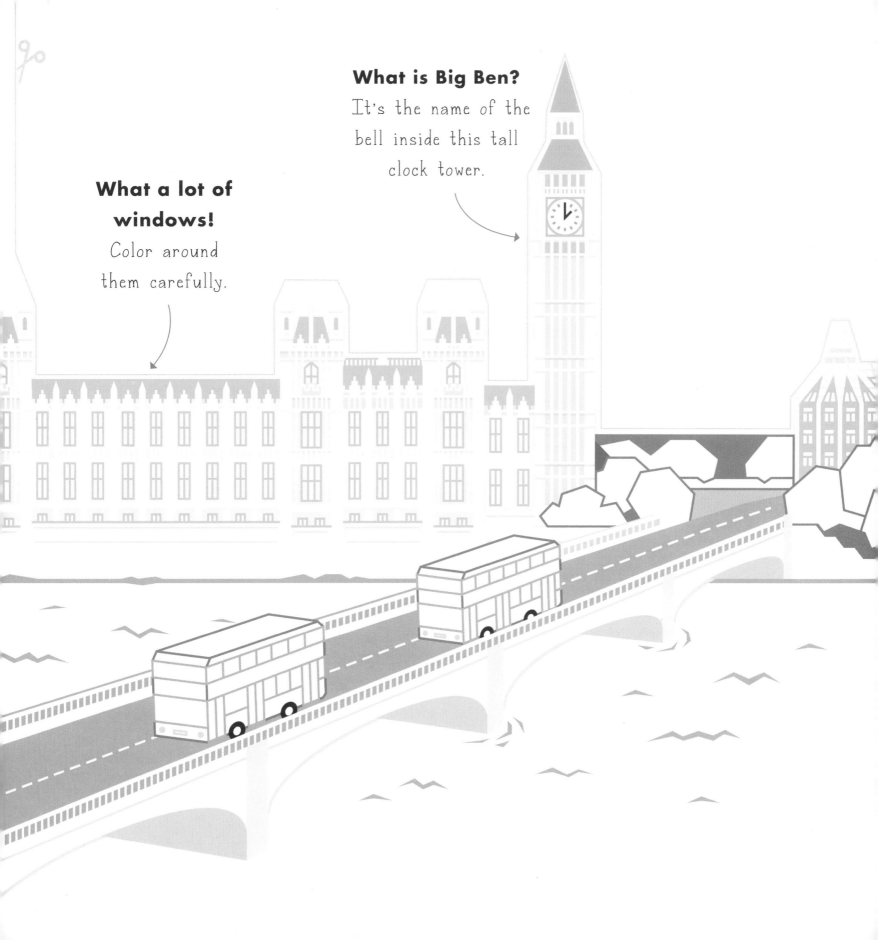

What is Big Ben?
It's the name of the bell inside this tall clock tower.

What a lot of windows!
Color around them carefully.

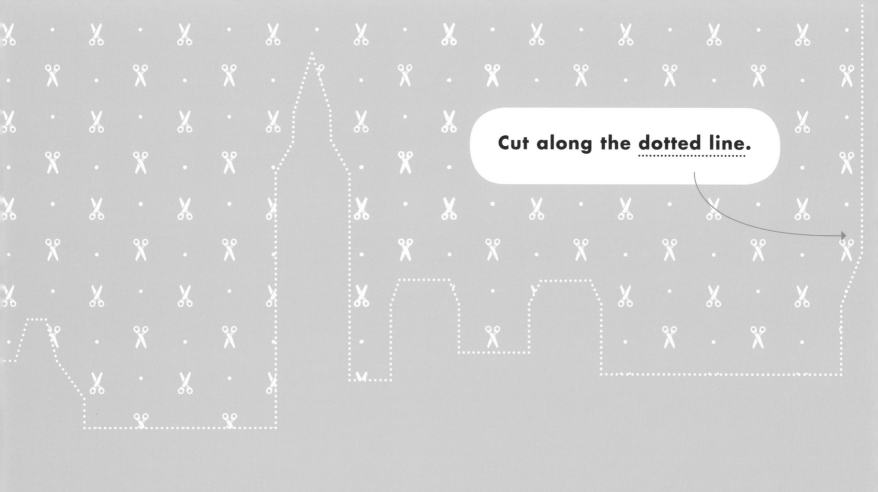

Cut along the **dotted line.**

The Tate

People from around the world visit this famous art gallery.

Are all the rowers wearing the same color?

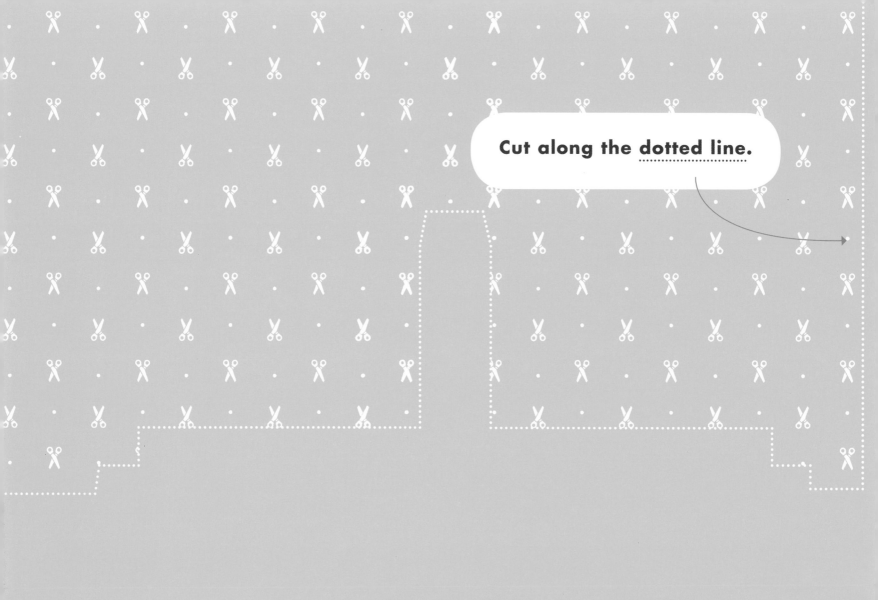

Cut along the dotted line.

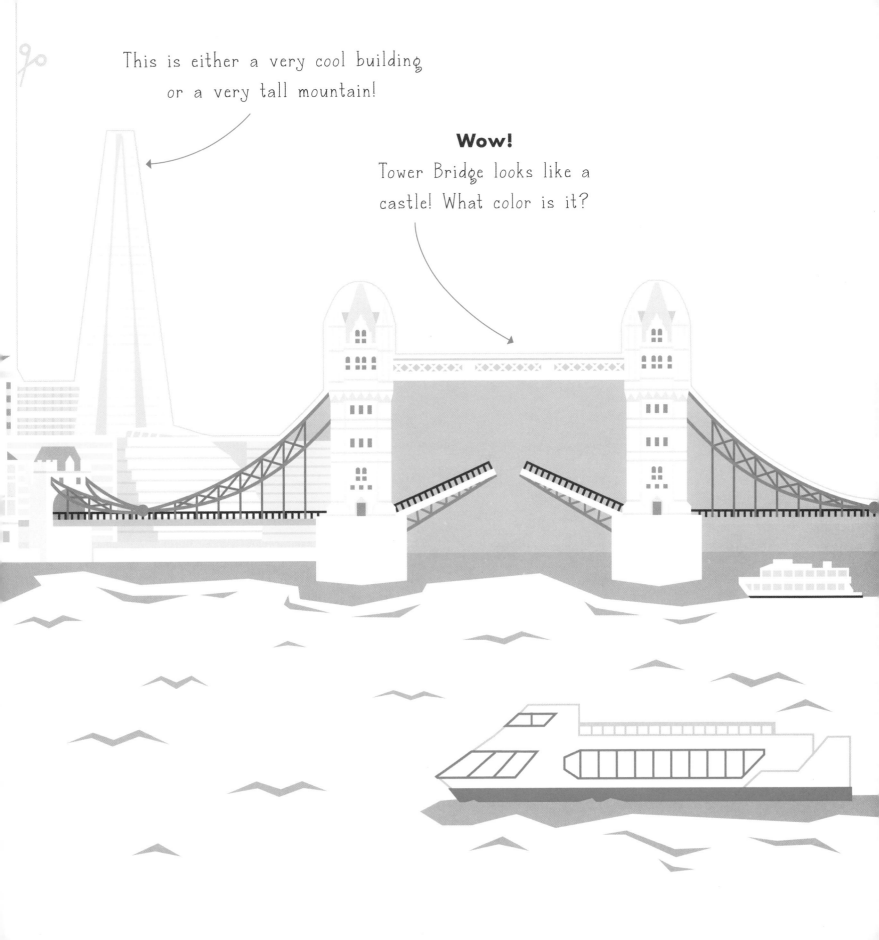

This is either a very cool building
or a very tall mountain!

Wow!
Tower Bridge looks like a
castle! What color is it?

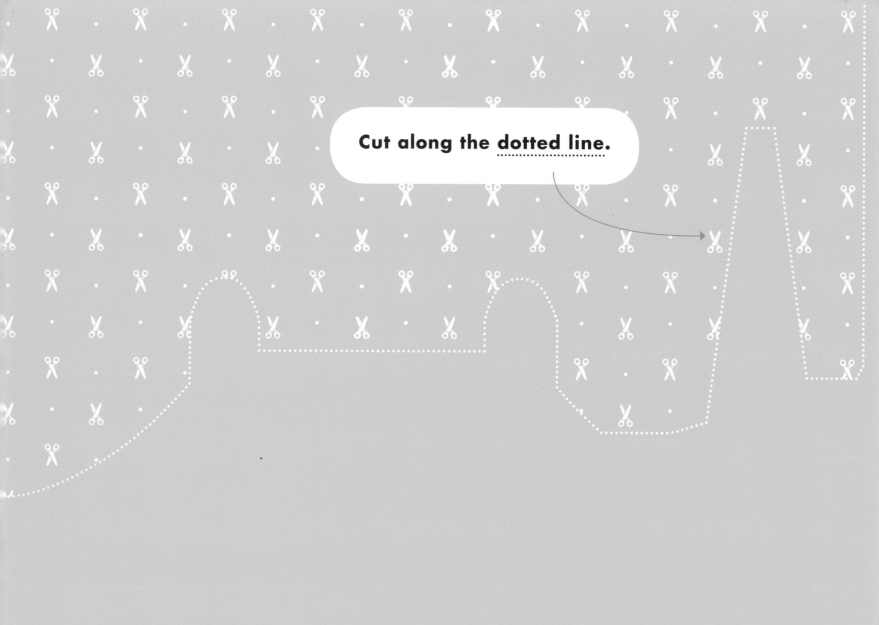

Cut along the <u>dotted line.</u>

These buildings are
different shapes and
sizes. What colors
are they?

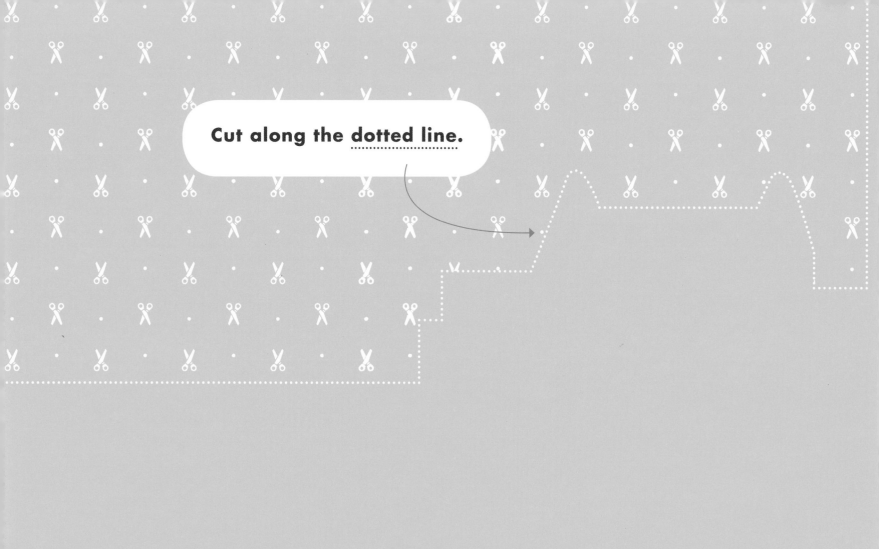

Cut along the dotted line.

PARIS

What a pretty city. There are narrow streets to explore, and little cafés, elegant parks and beautiful old buildings to visit.

Take care! It's very busy. People rush along the sidewalks. Buses, cars and motorcycles whizz along the main roads.

It's the weekend. People are enjoying the city. Families visit museums or stroll in the parks. The children sail toy boats in the fountain and play with their friends. The dogs have fun too!

Welcome to the city!

Choose your favorite
colors to make this frame
bright and exciting.

Start cutting here.

Splish splash...
Water flows from the
fountain into the pond. The
ripples glint in the sunshine.

Color in these trees with
different shades of green.

Cut along the dotted line.

Beep beep!
There are lots of cars on the road.
Where do you think they are going?

Cut along the dotted line.

Let's go shopping! Give this row of storefronts brightly striped awnings.

Cut along the dotted line.

What a lot of buildings!
Some of them are used as offices
and some are people's homes.

Cut along the dotted line.

Centre Pompidou

Can you see the museum among
the other buildings?

Spring is here!

Add green leaves and pretty
blossoms to the trees.

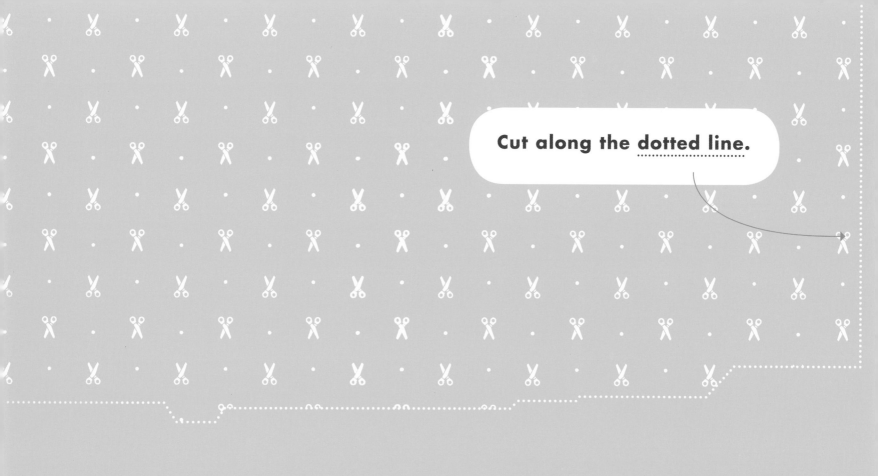

Cut along the dotted line.

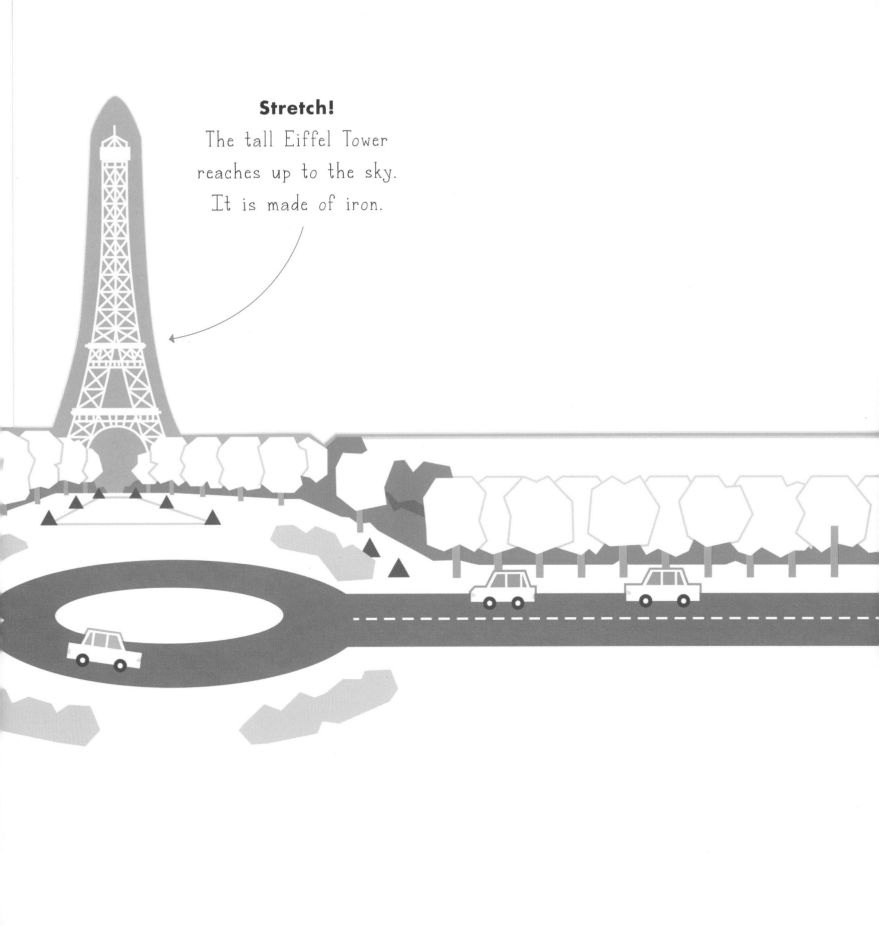

Stretch!

The tall Eiffel Tower
reaches up to the sky.
It is made of iron.

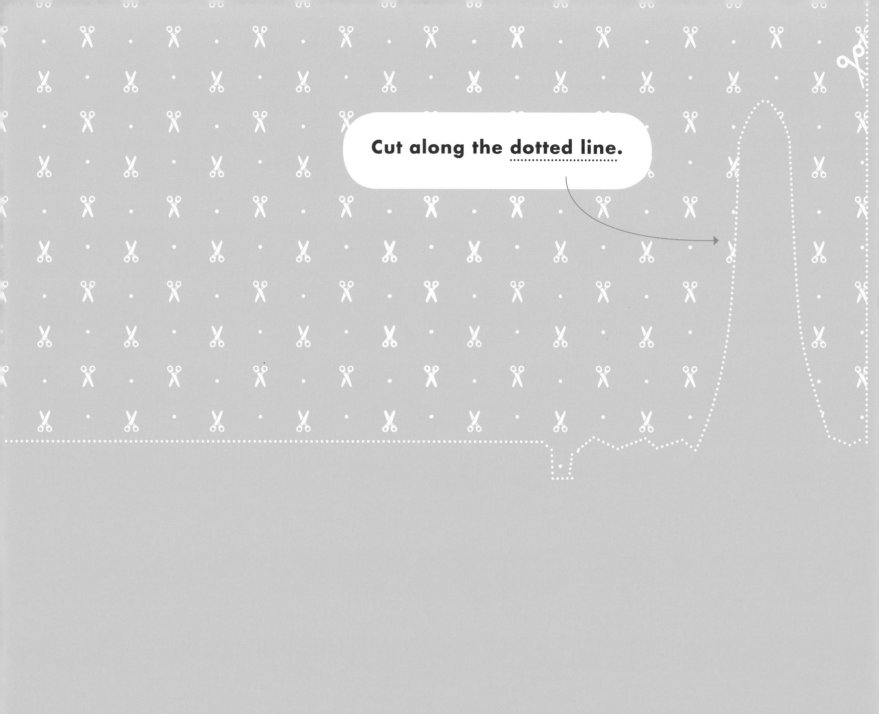

The pretty church of Sacré Coeur sits high on the hill. It has around 300 steps leading up to it.

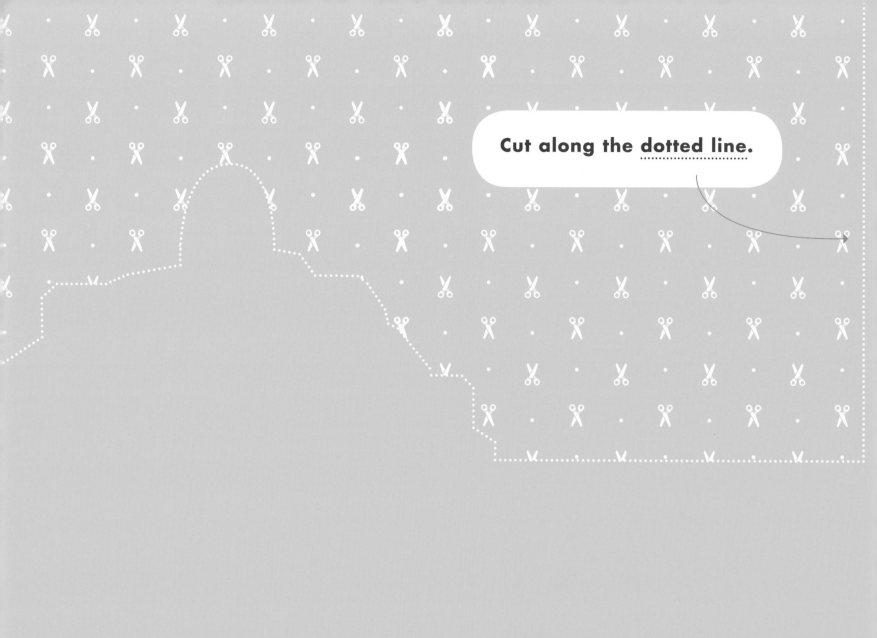

Cut along the dotted line.

Shaped like a spiral!

This skyscraper is called the Tour First and is the second-tallest building in Paris after the Eiffel Tower.

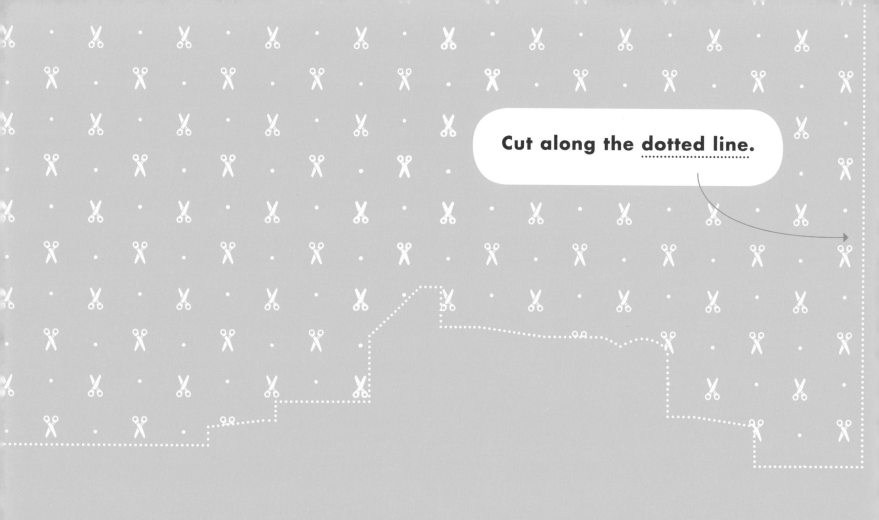

Cut along the dotted line.

NEW YORK

Woo-woo-woo! New York is a busy place! The bustling city streets are full of different sounds – people's voices, rushing traffic, honking horns and screaming sirens.

Wow! The tallest skyscrapers stretch high into the sky. Would you like to live in one? Imagine the view from the top – it must be awesome!

On hot days it's time to slow down. You can eat yummy ice cream in the shady park or cool off near the river.

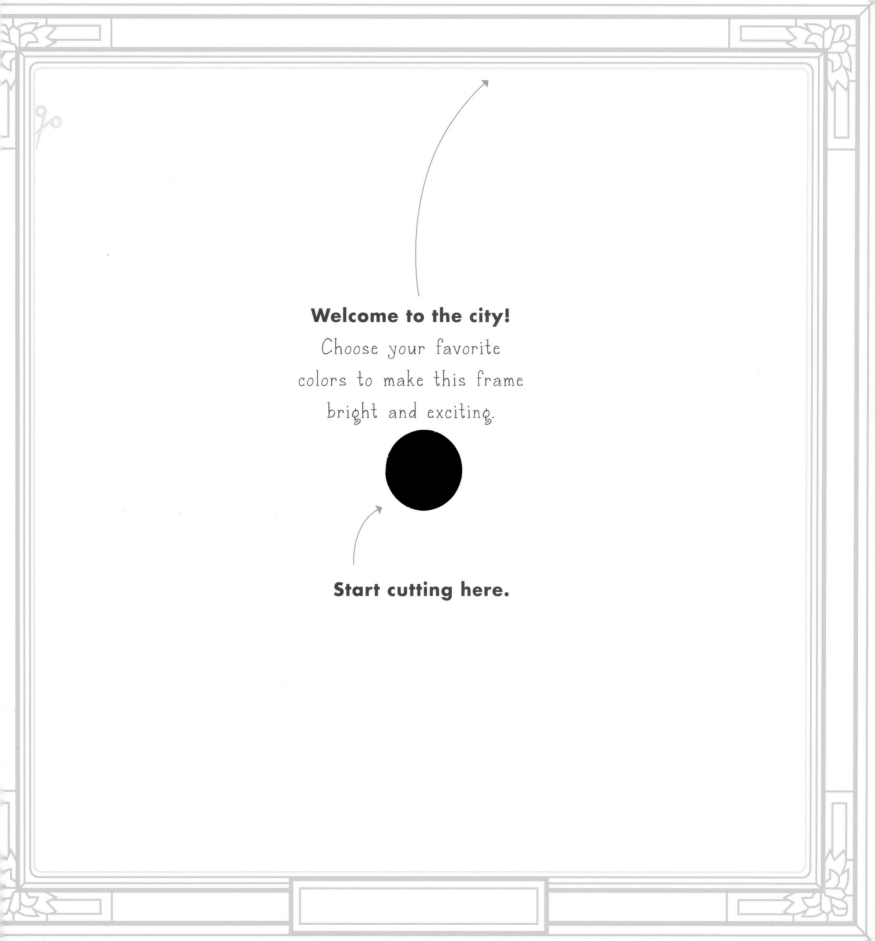

Welcome to the city!

Choose your favorite
colors to make this frame
bright and exciting.

Start cutting here.

Cut along the dotted line.

What an amazing statue!
This lady is called the Statue
of Liberty. She wears a crown
and holds a golden torch.

What color is this ferry?

Cut along the dotted line.

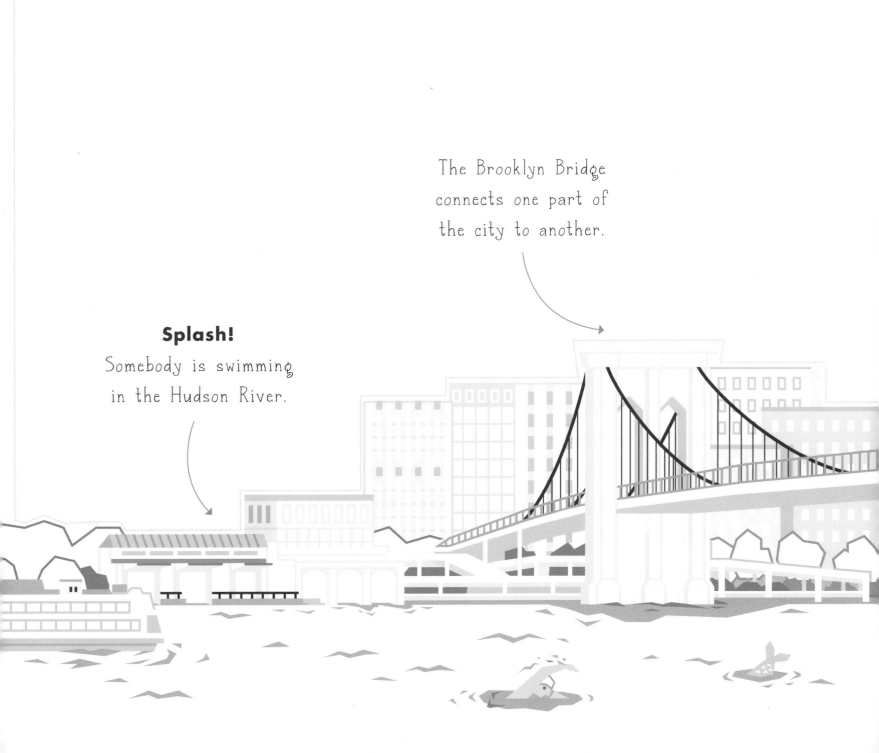

The Brooklyn Bridge
connects one part of
the city to another.

Splash!

Somebody is swimming
in the Hudson River.

Cut along the dotted line.

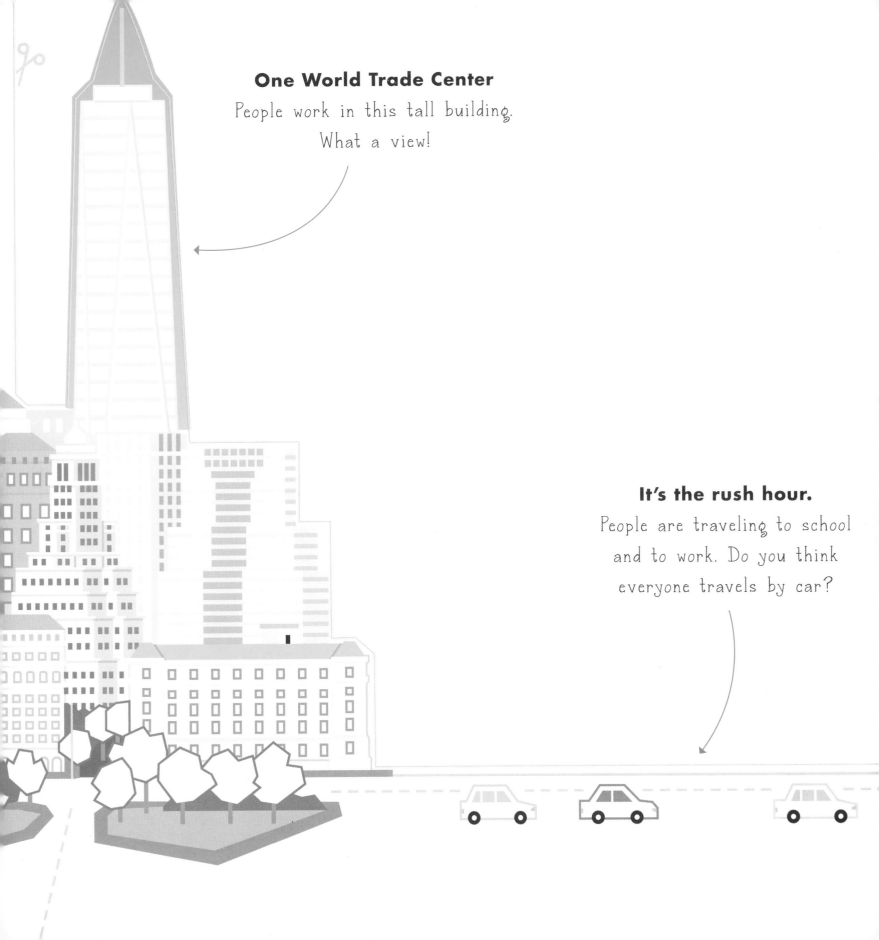

One World Trade Center
People work in this tall building.
What a view!

It's the rush hour.
People are traveling to school
and to work. Do you think
everyone travels by car?

What can you see on these houses? The zigzag steps on the outside are fire escapes. But some houses don't have an escape route—add them fast!

Color the water tanks on the roofs.

Cut along the dotted line.

The buildings lining this busy highway
are covered in billboards. Fill them in
with different colors and shapes.

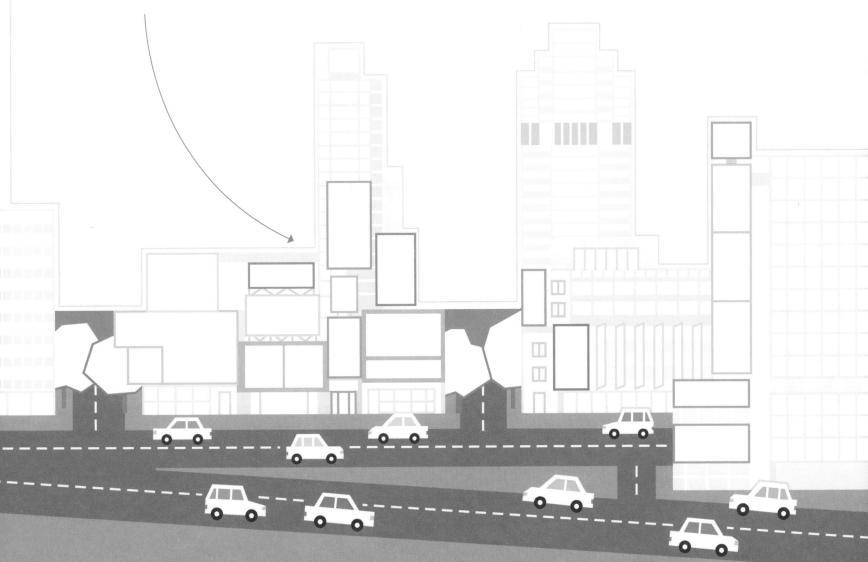

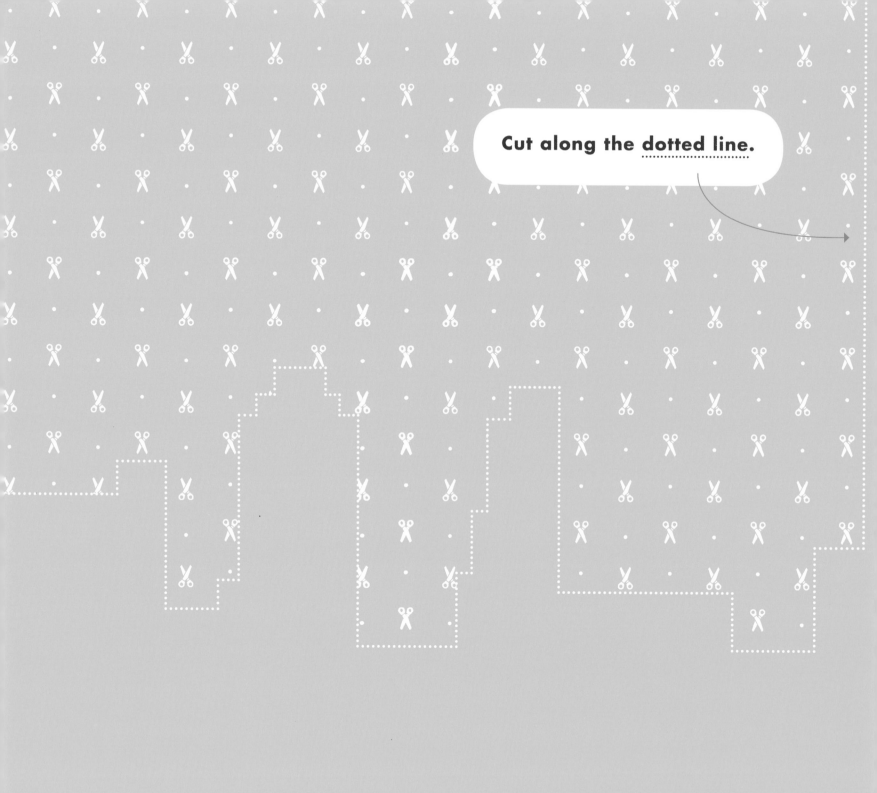

Cut along the dotted line.

Famous buildings.

These skyscrapers are famous in New York City.

This one is called the Chrysler Building.

This one is called the Empire State Building.

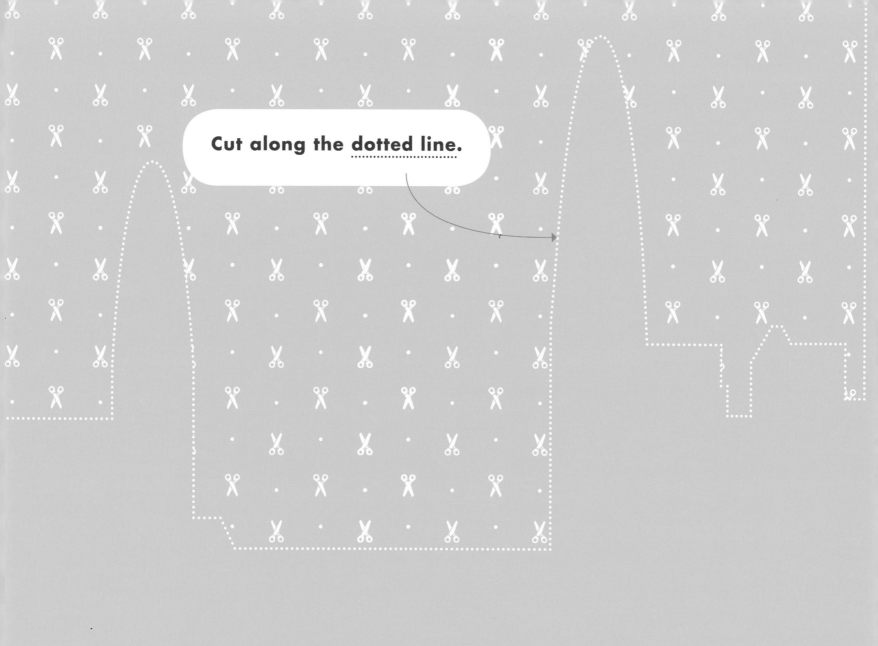

Cut along the dotted line.

It's a heat wave!
People are relaxing in the
park. Color their clothes
in summery shades.

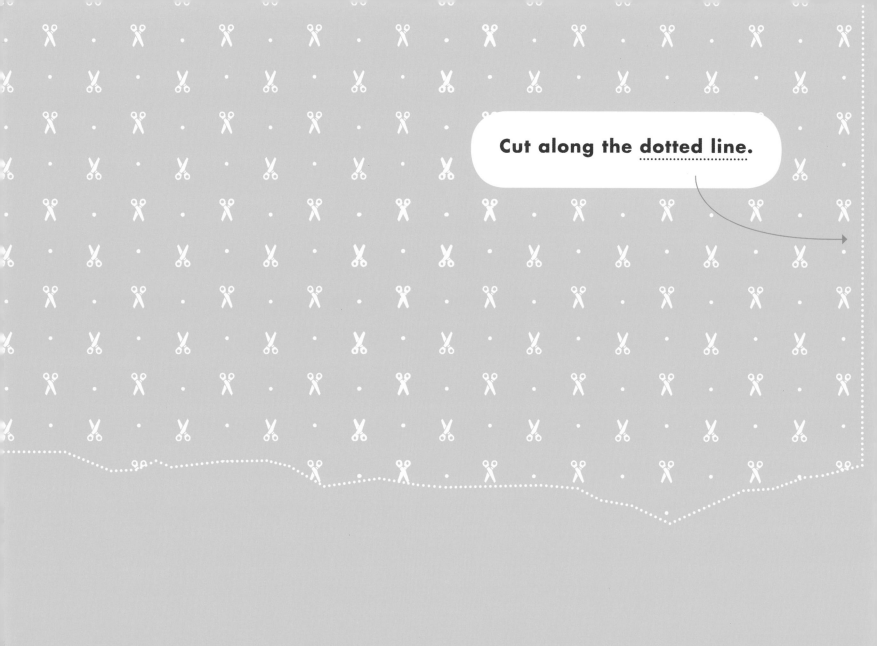

Cut along the dotted line.

Color each tree a
different shade of green.

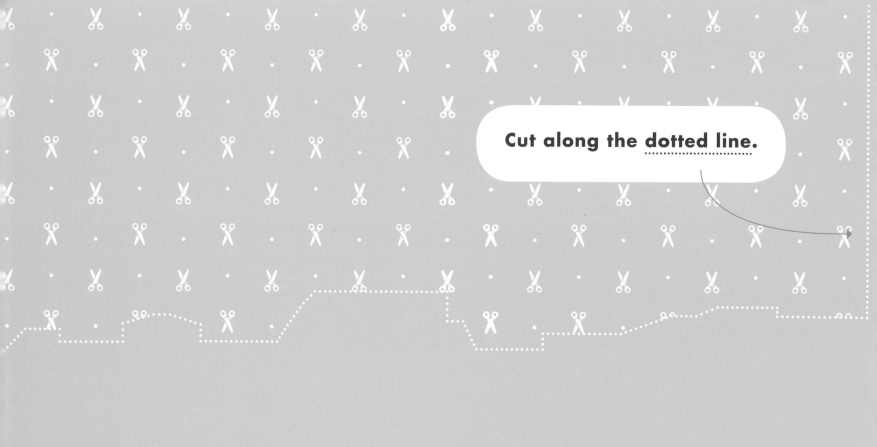

Cut along the dotted line.

MOSCOW

Brrr! It's very cold in the city. Everyone wears thick, warm clothes when they go out. It's easy to travel around by car, by bus or on foot.

The grand buildings look beautiful.

Some were once palaces! The shining golden domes and colorful decorations look magical in the snow.

Playtime! Playing in the snow is such fun. There is plenty of space in the city parks for building snowmen or for having a snowball fight!

Welcome to the city!

Choose your favorite
colors to make this frame
bright and exciting.

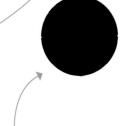

Start cutting here.

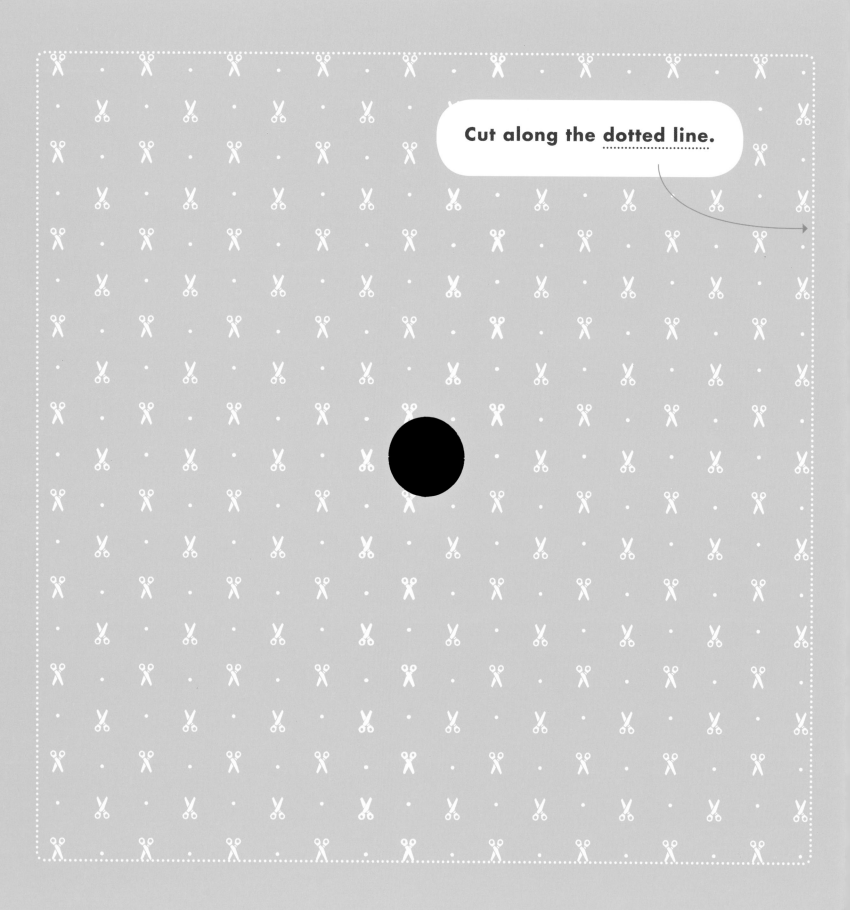

Cut along the dotted line.

Brrr!

It's a cold day today. The shoppers are dressed in warm, cozy clothes. Give them bright, colorful coats.

Cut along the dotted line.

What is this building?

This grand building is a
shopping mall! It has lots
of windows. Are the lights
on inside?

Can you see the little dog?
Make him brown and white.

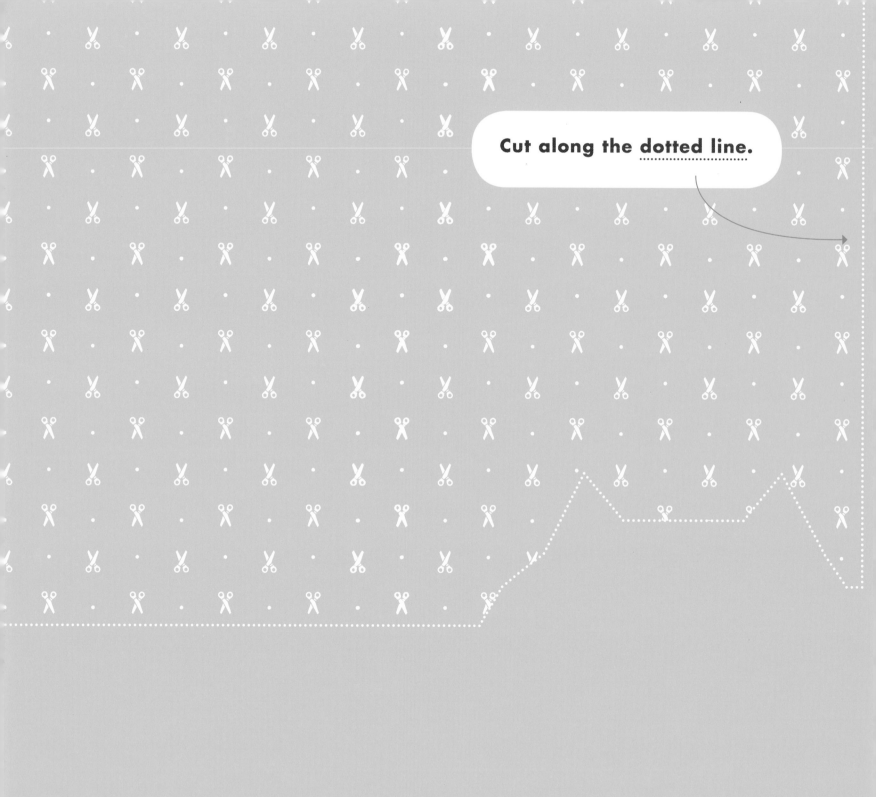

St. Basil's Cathedral has lots of domes. Color them green, red, yellow, blue and orange.

Make the rest of the building brown, gray and white.

Cut along the dotted line.

The Bolshoi Theatre

People go to the Bolshoi Theatre
to see ballets and operas.

Color in the trees and
bushes but remember
to add snow!

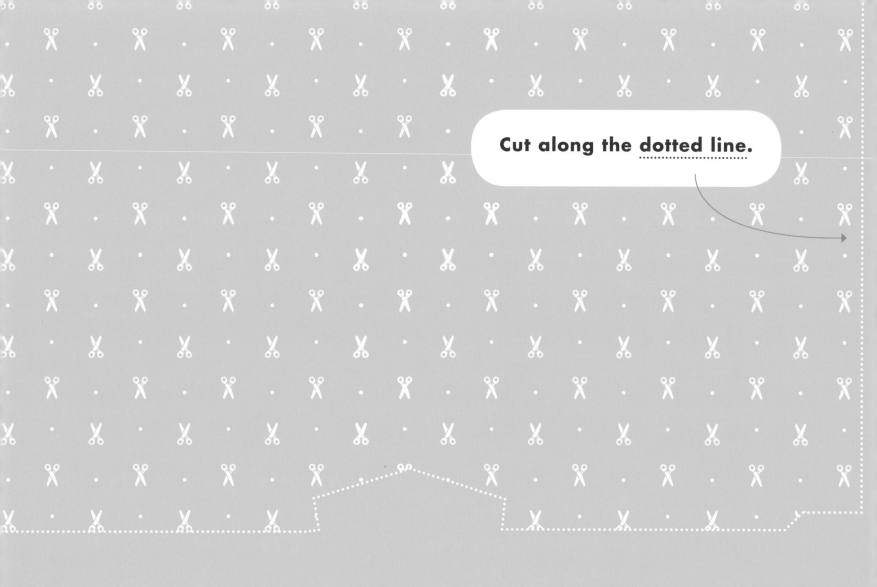

Cut along the dotted line.

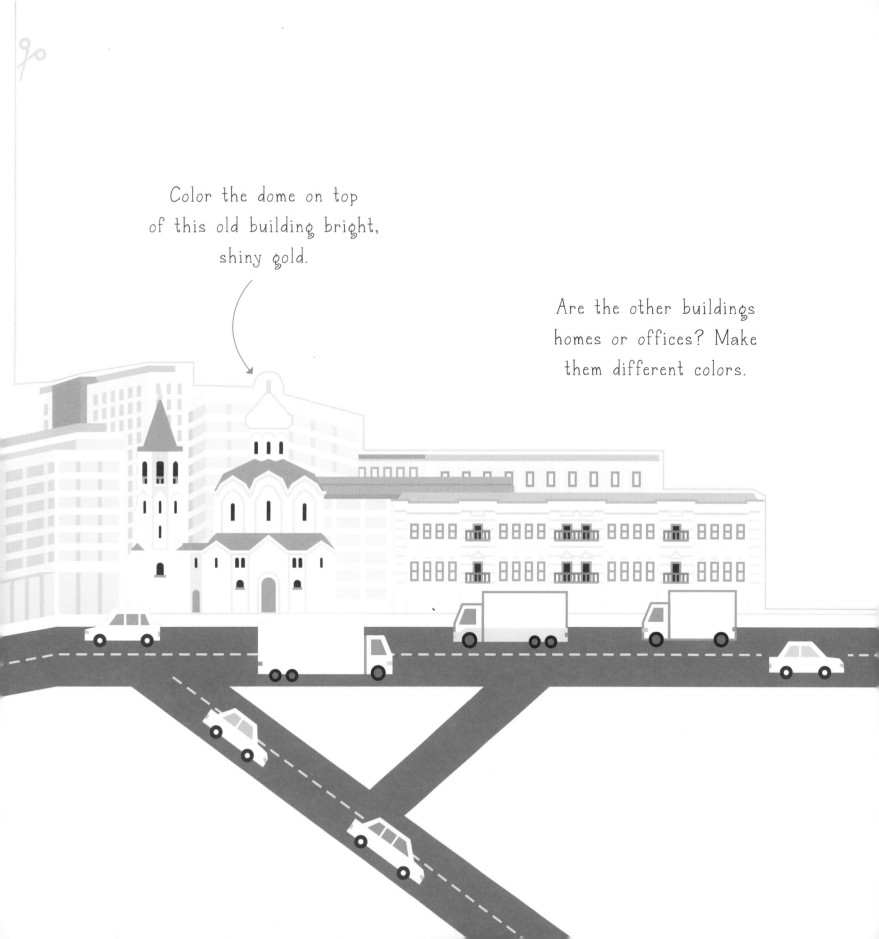

Color the dome on top
of this old building bright,
shiny gold.

Are the other buildings
homes or offices? Make
them different colors.

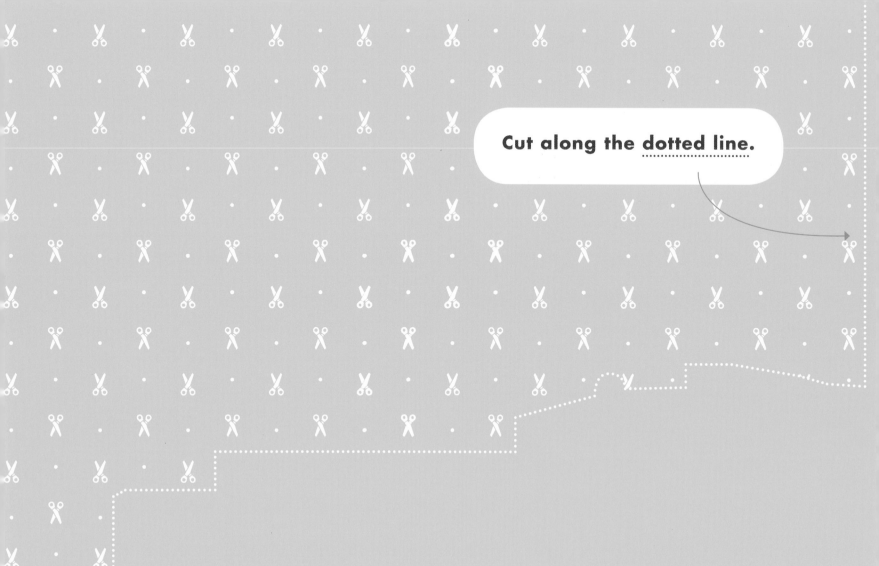

Cut along the dotted line.

Beep beep!

Delivery trucks are whizzing along
this highway at the edge of the city.
What do you think they are carrying?

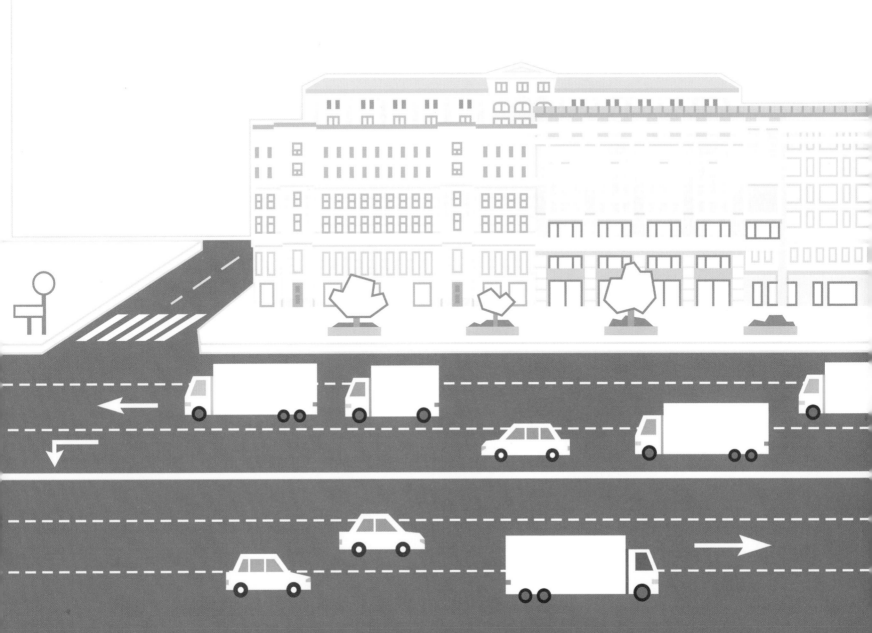

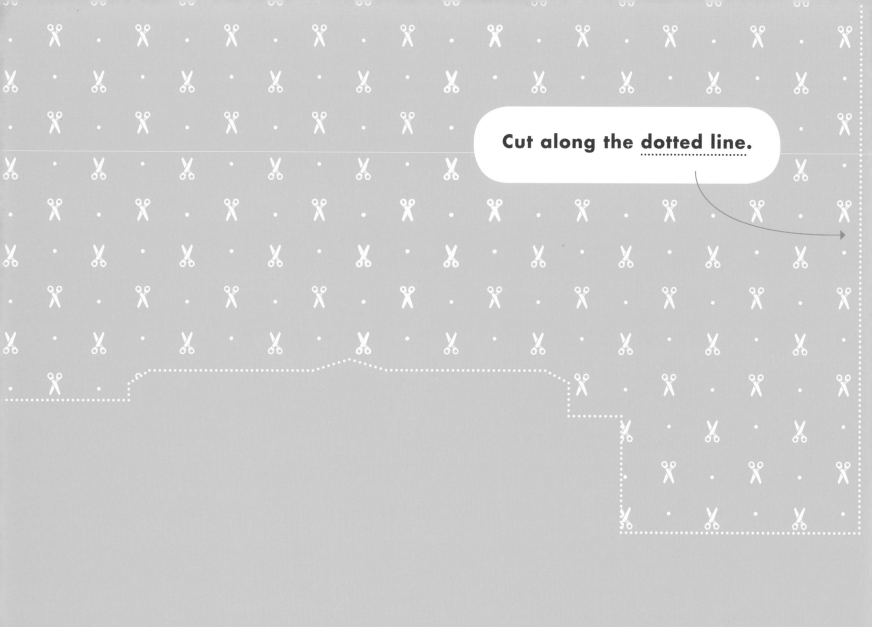

Cut along the dotted line.

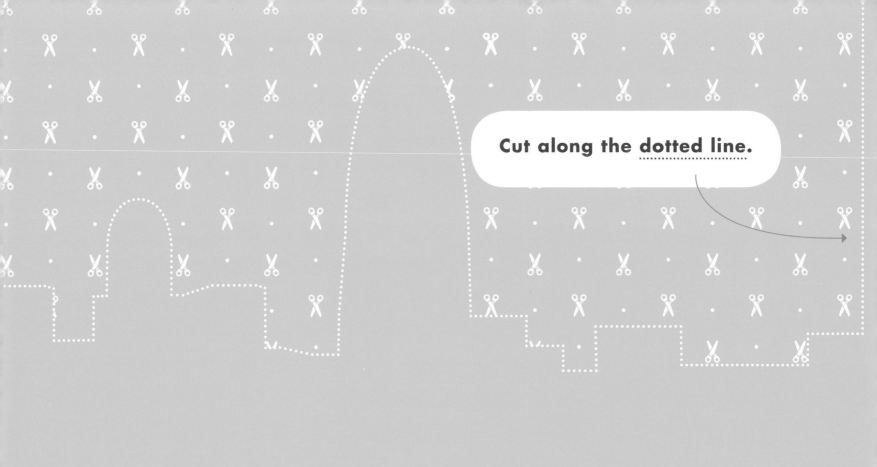

Cut along the dotted line.

Cut along the **dotted line.**

MAKE YOUR OWN THREE-LAYERED SCENE

Color, cut and create your own mini-city scene

1 Draw your own pictures in the spaces shown and then color them in.

2 Turn the pages over to see which parts to cut away. Any part of the paper with the scissor pattern must be cut away.

3 Flip back to the frame at the front to see your very own layered picture!

Tip: Try to draw bigger things at the front and smaller things at the back.

s your frame.

der around the edge

your favorite things.

cutting here.

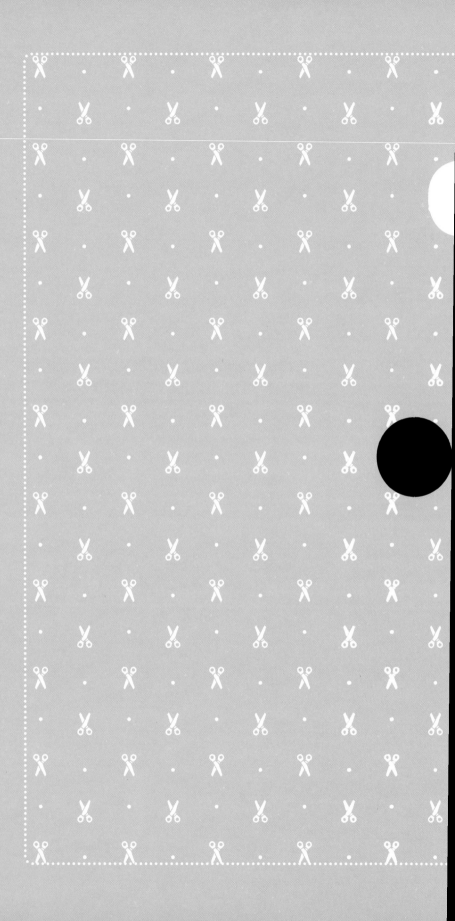

This is your frame.

Fill the border around the edge
with some of your favorite things.

Start cutting here.

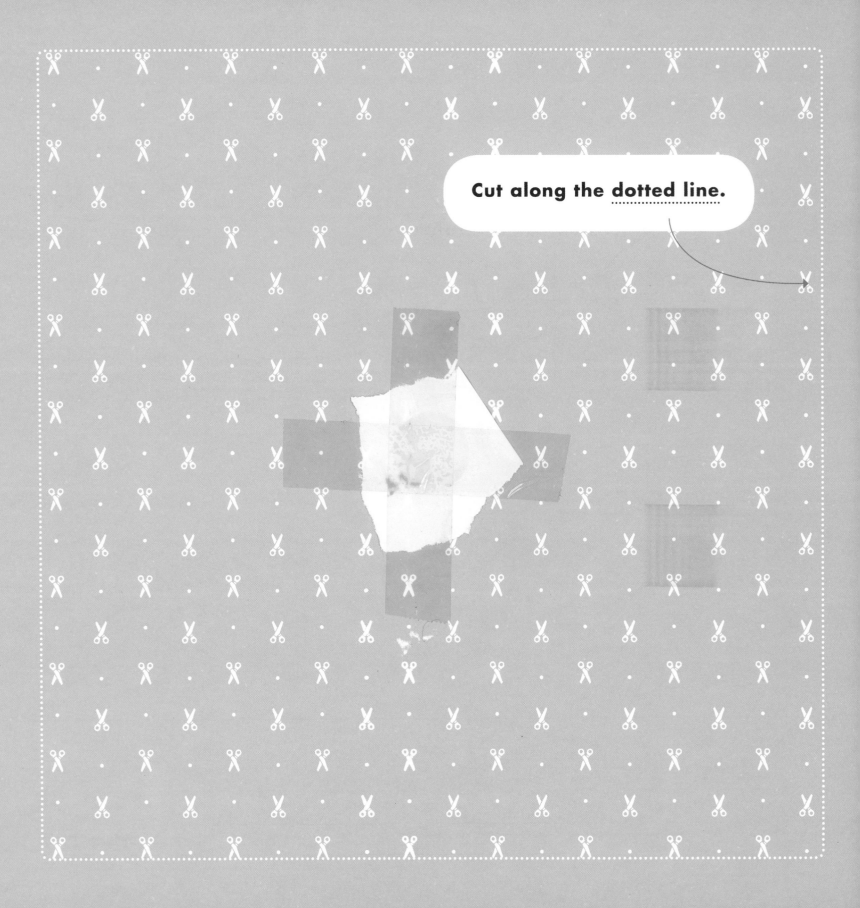

This is your first layer—a city park.

Draw trees, bushes, people and anything
else you like. This will be at the
front of your scene.

Cut along the dotted line.

This is your second layer.

Finish drawing the buildings, then add roads and cars in the middle of the page so you can see them above the first layer.

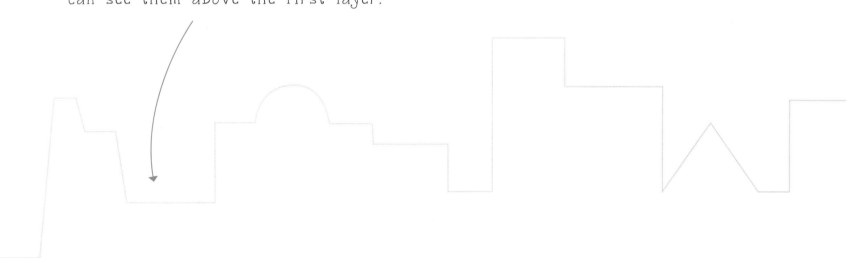

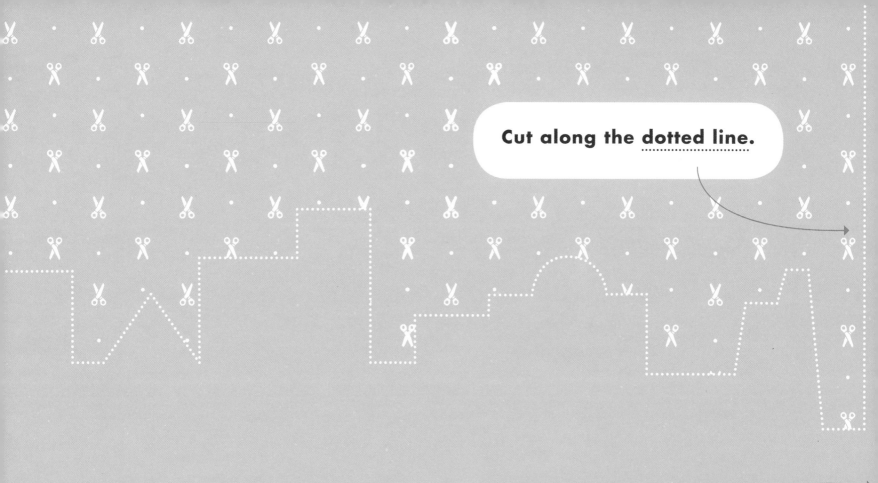

Cut along the dotted line.

**This is the back
of your scene.**
Draw something at the
top part of this page so
you can see it above
the other layers.

YOUR DESIGNS

96